Short Stories of Might and Magic

George Gentle

Published by George Gentle, 2024.

This is a work of fiction. Similarities to real people, places, or events are entirely coincidental.

SHORT STORIES OF MIGHT AND MAGIC

First edition. July 8, 2024.

Copyright © 2024 George Gentle.

ISBN: 979-8227257093

Written by George Gentle.

Chapter 1: The Halls of Valhalla.

LEIF STORM RIDER, A fearless and renowned Viking warrior, stood tall among his brethren on the battlefield. With his mighty axe in hand and the wind at his back, he fought with a ferocity unmatched by any other. The clash of swords, the screams of the fallen, and the thunderous roars of warriors echoed throughout the land. But fate had other plans for Leif that day. As he valiantly fought, a spear pierced his side, and he fell to the ground, his lifeblood staining the earth beneath him. The battle continued, but Leif's spirit soared high above, carried by the Valkyries to the grand halls of Valhalla.

In the grand halls of Valhalla, Leif Storm Rider found himself surrounded by the spirits of fallen warriors. The air was thick with the scent of mead and the sound of boisterous laughter, as warriors from all corners of the world celebrated their glorious deaths.

Leif's eyes widened as he beheld the magnificent sight before him. The hall was adorned with golden tapestries depicting ancient battles and heroic deeds. The walls were lined with shields and weapons, each one bearing the mark of a legendary warrior. The ceiling, high above, seemed to stretch into eternity, with celestial lights twinkling like stars.

As Leif took in his surroundings, he noticed a figure approaching him. It was a Valkyrie, her wings shimmering with an otherworldly glow. Her eyes held a wisdom that surpassed mortal understanding, and her presence commanded respect.

"Leif Storm Rider," she spoke with a voice that resonated through his very soul, "you have fought with unmatched courage and valor on the battlefield. Your name echoes through the annals of Viking history. You have earned your place in Valhalla."

Leif bowed his head, humbled by the words of the Valkyrie. "It is an honor to stand among such legendary warriors," he replied, his voice filled with gratitude.

The Valkyrie smiled, her eyes gleaming with pride. "Indeed, you have earned your place here. But the battles do not end on Midgard. Here in Valhalla, you will train and prepare for the final battle, Ragnarok. The fate of the gods and mortals alike rests on the shoulders of those who dwell within these halls."

Leif nodded, understanding the weight of the Valkyrie's words. He had heard tales of Ragnarok, the apocalyptic battle that would determine the fate of the Nine Realms. It was a battle that would test the strength and resolve of every warrior in Valhalla.

As Leif settled into his new existence in Valhalla, he immersed himself in the training and camaraderie that filled the halls. The days were spent honing his skills, sparring with fellow warriors, and learning from the ancient gods who resided in Valhalla. The nights were filled with feasting and storytelling, as warriors shared their tales of glory and conquest.

But amidst the revelry and training, Leif couldn't shake the memories of the battle that had brought him to Valhalla. He thought of his brethren who had fought alongside him, their faces etched in his mind. He wondered if they too had found their way to these hallowed halls.

One day, as he wandered through the vast courtyard of Valhalla, Leif came across a familiar face. It was Bjorn Ironheart, his closest friend and comrade in battle. Bjorn's eyes lit up with joy as he spotted Leif, and they embraced like brothers long separated.

"Leif, my brother! I had feared we would never see each other again," Bjorn exclaimed, his voice filled with relief.

Leif smiled, his heart swelling with happiness at the sight of his friend. "Bjorn, it is good to see you. I had hoped we would find each other in Valhalla."

Bjorn nodded, his gaze wandering to the countless warriors training around them. "Indeed, my friend. But now we must prepare for

Ragnarok. The final battle approaches, and we must be ready to face whatever challenges lie ahead."

Leif's determination flared within him, fueled by the prospect of Ragnarok. He knew that the battles he had fought on Midgard were but a taste of the ultimate conflict that awaited them. With Bjorn by his side, he vowed to train harder, to become a warrior worthy of the gods' blessings.

And so, in the grand halls of Valhalla, Leif Storm Rider and Bjorn Ironheart prepared for the battle that would determine the fate of the Nine Realms. As their swords clashed and their spirits soared, they knew that their journey was far from over.

Chapter 2: The Call of Destiny.

IN VALHALLA, LEIF FOUND himself immersed in a grand spectacle of bravery and camaraderie. The great hall echoed with the boisterous merriment of warriors, their voices intermingling with the clinking of goblets and the hearty laughter that filled the air. The mead flowed freely, a symbol of the eternal bliss that awaited those who had proven their mettle on the battlefield.

Amidst the revelry, Leif noticed a figure approaching him. As he turned to face the newcomer, his heart skipped a beat. It was Odin, the Allfather, the ruler of the gods. The imposing presence of the god of war and wisdom commanded attention, and the air seemed to crackle with anticipation.

Odin's voice resonated with authority as he addressed Leif, his words carrying the weight of centuries. "Warrior," he began, his voice resounding like thunder, "your valor on the battlefield has caught my eye. You have demonstrated exceptional skill and unwavering courage. I offer you a choice, one that few mortals have been granted. You may return to the mortal realm as an immortal instrument of the gods, or you may remain in Valhalla, basking in eternal glory."

Leif's heart swelled with a mixture of pride and purpose. He had always felt a deep yearning for something greater than himself, a desire to leave a lasting mark on the world. The prospect of becoming an immortal, a champion of the gods, ignited a fire within him. He knew that his destiny lay beyond the golden gates of Valhalla, beckoning him to a path of greatness.

With unwavering determination, Leif stepped forward, his eyes meeting Odin's gaze. "I accept your offer, Allfather," he declared, his voice filled with conviction. "I am ready to embrace this new chapter of my existence, to become an immortal servant of the gods. I will wield my skills and bravery to protect and honor the realms, to ensure that the legacy of the gods endures for eternity."

As his words hung in the air, a sense of purpose washed over Leif. He knew that the path he had chosen would be fraught with challenges and sacrifices, but he was prepared to face them head-on. With the gods' favor bestowed upon him, he would embark on a journey that would test his limits, push him to the brink, and ultimately shape him into a legendary figure of myth and legend.

And so, in that moment, Leif's fate was sealed. He would leave behind the revelry and camaraderie of Valhalla, venturing forth into the mortal realm as an immortal instrument of the gods. With the blessings of Odin and the weight of destiny upon his shoulders, he would carve his name into the annals of history, forever remembered as a hero who answered the call of the gods.

Chapter 3: The Rainbow Bridge.

LEIF STEPPED OUT OF the great hall, feeling a surge of excitement and anticipation. He was greeted by a magnificent sight: a winged steed, white as snow, with a golden mane and tail. The creature was a gift from Odin, a means of transportation and a loyal companion for his immortal journey. Leif approached the steed, admiring its beauty and grace. He felt a connection with the animal, as if they shared a bond of trust and respect.

He mounted the steed, feeling its powerful muscles tense beneath him. He looked up at the sky, where a rainbow bridge spanned the horizon. The bridge was the Bifröst, the gateway between the realms of gods and men. Leif knew that he had to cross it, to leave behind the realm of Asgard and enter the realm of Midgard, where his destiny awaited him.

He urged the steed forward, feeling a rush of wind in his face. The steed took off, soaring into the air with a majestic flap of its wings. Leif felt a thrill of exhilaration as he flew towards the rainbow bridge, leaving behind the golden spires of Valhalla. He looked ahead, where a new world beckoned him, a world full of wonders and dangers, challenges and opportunities, glory and honor.

Leif crossed the Bifröst, feeling a jolt of energy as he entered the realm of Midgard. He looked down, seeing a vast and diverse landscape below him. He saw mountains and valleys, forests and fields, rivers and lakes, villages and cities. He saw people of different races and cultures, living in harmony or conflict, depending on the region. He saw signs of progress and innovation, as well as decay and corruption. He saw a world that was both familiar and foreign to him, a world that needed his help.

Chapter 4: Astrid Frostheart.

LEIF HAD ALWAYS KNOWN that his return to Earth would come with its own set of challenges. As an immortal being, he was acutely aware of the passing of time and the inevitable ageing that mortals experienced. But he was determined to make the most of his time on Earth and embrace the joys and sorrows that came with mortal life. Settling in a small village on the outskirts of the fjords, Leif found solace in the simplicity of the countryside. The rolling hills and vast landscapes reminded him of the beauty he had witnessed in the realms of the gods. It was here that he met Astrid Frostheart, a strong and beautiful woman who captured his heart from the moment he laid eyes on her. Astrid was unlike anyone Leif had ever met. Her spirit was as fierce as the winds that swept through the fjords, and her heart was as warm as the hearth in their humble farmstead. They shared a love that was both tender and fierce, and together they built a life that was filled with love, laughter, and hard work.

Their farmstead became a symbol of their dreams and aspirations. They sowed the seeds of their labor, tending to the fields with care and dedication. Leif reveled in the simple pleasures of watching the crops grow and the animals thrive. It was a reminder of the cycle of life and the beauty of nature that he had witnessed in the realms of the gods, together, they faced the joys and sorrows that life threw their way. They weathered storms and celebrated harvests. And through it all Leif and Astrid found solace in their love for each other and the life they had built together. They embraced the fleeting nature of mortal existence, cherishing each moment and treasuring the memories they created. Leif knew that his time with Astrid was limited, but he was determined to make every second count. His immortality served as a constant reminder of the fragility of mortal life. It was a gift and a curse, a reminder of the sacrifices he had made and the love he had found. But he wouldn't trade it for anything in the world. For in the arms of Astrid, he had found a love that transcended time and mortality. And in the small village on the outskirts of the fjords, they lived a life that was filled with love, purpose, and the beauty of being mortal.

Chapter 5: The Call of Odin.

ONE FATEFUL NIGHT, as Leif slumbered peacefully, a vivid dream visited him, transporting him to a realm beyond the mortal plane. In this ethereal world, Odin, the Allfather of the gods, materialized before him, his presence emanating an aura of power and urgency. The sound of his voice reverberated through Leif's very being.

"Leif Storm Rider," Odin boomed, his voice a thunderous symphony, "the time has come for you to rise to your destiny. A great darkness looms, threatening to engulf the realms and plunge them into eternal chaos. Thornheart, a vile troll of immense power, seeks to raise an army of darkness to wage war on the gods themselves."

Leif's heart raced as he absorbed the weight of Odin's words. He realised that he was being called upon to fulfill a purpose greater than himself. He was to be the instrument of the gods' will, the chosen one destined to stand against Thornheart and his malevolent plans.

Awakening from his dream, Leif found himself drenched in a cold sweat, his heart pounding with newfound determination. The call of Odin had ignited a fire within him, urging him to embark on a perilous journey to protect the realms from the impending threat.

With Astrid, his steadfast companion, by his side, Leif shared his divine encounter. She listened intently, her eyes ablaze with unwavering support and belief in his destiny. Together, they vowed to face the challenges ahead, united in their dedication to safeguarding the realms from Thornheart's maleficence. The path ahead was treacherous and fraught with danger, but Leif and Astrid were undeterred. They knew that the fate of the realms rested upon their shoulders, and they would not falter in the face of adversity.

Leif and Astrid began their journey by seeking guidance from the wise seers and sages scattered across the realms. They traveled through enchanted forests, climbed towering mountains, and crossed vast oceans, seeking the knowledge and power they needed to confront Thornheart.

Each encounter with the seers brought them closer to understanding the true extent of Thornheart's darkness. They learned of his ability to manipulate the very fabric of reality, his mastery over dark magic, and his insatiable hunger for power. It became clear that defeating him would require more than just physical strength; it would require cunning, strategy, and the unity of all the realms.

Chapter 6: A Quest for Allies.

LEIF'S JOURNEY LED him through a myriad of treacherous landscapes, each presenting its own set of challenges. His first stop was the icy mountains, where he hoped to find the powerful Frost Giants. These giants were known for their immense strength and ability to control the freezing temperatures of their surroundings. Leif knew that their assistance would be crucial in his quest to defeat the malevolent sorcerer who threatened his homeland.

Navigating through the treacherous icy terrain was no easy feat. Leif had to endure bone-chilling temperatures and slippery slopes, constantly on the lookout for avalanches and hidden crevasses. After days of arduous climbing, he finally reached the lair of the Frost Giants.

To gain their trust, Leif had to prove his worthiness. He engaged in a brutal battle with their strongest warrior, a towering giant with icy blue skin and a massive ice hammer. The fight tested Leif's strength, agility, and strategic thinking. After a grueling duel, Leif emerged victorious, earning the respect and alliance of the Frost Giants.

Leaving the icy mountains behind, Leif ventured into the dense forests, where he encountered a whole new set of challenges. The forest was home to mystical creatures like the Wood Nymphs, mischievous beings who possessed the ability to manipulate nature. Leif sought their aid in navigating the enchanted forest, as their knowledge of the land was unparalleled.

However, the Wood Nymphs were notorious for their distrust of humans. Leif had to prove his intentions were pure and gain their trust. He embarked on a quest to retrieve a rare flower that bloomed only once every hundred years. This flower held great significance to the Wood Nymphs, as it possessed healing properties that could save their dying queen.

Leif's journey through the dense forest was fraught with danger. He encountered venomous snakes, treacherous quicksand, and deceptive illusions that tested his resolve. But his determination never wavered, and he overcame each obstacle with unwavering perseverance.

After days of searching, Leif finally found the elusive flower. Presenting it to the Wood Nymphs, he earned their gratitude and secured their alliance. With their guidance, he traversed the labyrinthine paths of the enchanted forest, avoiding traps and pitfalls that could have easily ensnared him.

Leif's encounters with allies and mythical creatures were not without their trials. These challenges tested his physical and mental strength, as well as his ability to adapt to unfamiliar environments. But with each victory, Leif grew more confident, knowing that he was one step closer to fulfilling his quest.

Chapter 7: The Battle for Light.

THE FROST GIANTS AND Wood Nymphs stood beside Leif, their determination evident in their eyes. They had come together, united by a common purpose - to protect their lands from the encroaching darkness that Thornheart represented. The giants, towering over the battlefield, brandished their massive ice hammers, ready to unleash their fury upon the enemy. The nymphs, graceful and ethereal, held their bows and arrows, their aim true and deadly.

Leif took a deep breath, his heart pounding with anticipation. He knew that this battle would not only determine the fate of their realm but also test the strength of their convictions. He had seen the devastation Thornheart had wrought upon innocent villages, the pain and suffering he had inflicted upon the innocent. Leif could not stand idly by while evil reigned.

Thornheart, a grotesque creature with gnarled horns protruding from his head, sneered at Leif and his allies. His eyes glowed with a sickly green light, a reflection of the darkness that consumed his soul. He raised his massive club, covered in spikes and dripping with venom, ready to strike fear into the hearts of his opponents.

Leif's grip tightened around his sword, a weapon forged from the purest essence of light. It hummed with power, resonating with his immortal energy. He knew that his strength alone would not be enough to defeat Thornheart. It would require the combined might of the Frost Giants and the Wood Nymphs, their unity and unwavering belief in the cause.

With a nod, Leif signaled his allies to advance. The ground shook beneath their feet as they charged towards Thornheart and his forces. The clash of steel against steel echoed through the air, mingling with the cries of battle and the roars of the giants. Arrows whistled through the sky, finding their mark with deadly precision.

Leif's sword danced through the chaos, its radiant light cutting through the darkness that surrounded them. He fought with a purpose, his every strike fueled by the desire to protect the innocent and restore peace to their lands. The Frost Giants unleashed their icy wrath, freezing the enemy in their tracks, while the Wood Nymphs used their magic to ensnare and confound their foes.

But Thornheart was no ordinary troll. He possessed a cunning intellect and a resilience that matched his malevolence. He swung his club with a ferocity that shook the very earth, his blows leaving destruction in their wake. He reveled in the chaos, feeding off the fear and despair of those who opposed him.

As the battle raged on, Leif's determination grew stronger. He could not allow Thornheart to prevail, to continue spreading his darkness across their realm. With a surge of power, he unleashed a wave of light that engulfed the battlefield, momentarily blinding his enemies. In that moment, Leif's allies seized the opportunity, striking with renewed vigor.

The clash of ideologies intensified, the battle becoming a struggle for the very soul of their realm. Leif and his allies fought with every ounce of strength they possessed, their belief in the power of good propelling them forward. They knew that the outcome of this battle would shape the future of their world, and they were prepared to give everything they had to ensure that light triumphed over darkness.

Chapter 8: Leif's Triumph over Thornheart.

LEIF'S BATTLE WITH Thornheart was not just a physical confrontation, but a clash of ideologies and the embodiment of good versus evil. As they faced off, the air crackled with energy, and the ground trembled beneath their feet. Leif's immortal powers radiated from him, a brilliant aura of light that contrasted sharply with Thornheart's dark and malevolent presence.

Thornheart, with his twisted and gnarled form, wielded dark magic with a sinister grace. He conjured spells that sent waves of destruction hurtling towards Leif, but the immortal hero deftly dodged and countered, his movements fluid and precise. Leif's powers, rooted in purity and righteousness, acted as a shield against Thornheart's malevolence, and each clash of their forces sent shockwaves rippling through the battlefield. The battle raged on, with Leif summoning the elements to aid him. Thunder roared overhead, lightning crackled through the air, and gusts of wind whipped around them. Thornheart, however, was no ordinary foe. He unleashed his own dark forces, summoning shadowy creatures and casting spells that twisted reality itself. The battlefield became a chaotic maelstrom of light and darkness, with Leif's unyielding determination driving him forward.

As the battle intensified, Leif tapped into the depths of his immortal powers. He drew strength from the love and hope of the realms he protected, channeling that energy into a devastating attack. A blinding beam of pure light shot forth from his outstretched hand, piercing through Thornheart's defenses and striking him directly. The malevolent troll howled in pain as the light burned away his dark magic, weakening him.

With Thornheart weakened, Leif pressed his advantage. He closed in, striking blow after blow with his sword, each strike fueled by his unwavering resolve. Thornheart fought back, using every ounce of his remaining power, but it was not enough. Leif's determination and his connection to the realms he protected gave him an edge that Thornheart could not match.

Finally, with one last mighty swing of his sword, Leif struck Thornheart down. The malevolent troll let out a final, agonized roar before crumbling into dust, his dark army dissipating alongside him. The realms were saved, and the gods looked down in awe at their champion's triumph.

Leif stood victorious amidst the wreckage of the battlefield, his immortal powers still radiating from him. He had faced the embodiment of evil and emerged triumphant, his determination and unwavering spirit prevailing against all odds. The realms were safe once more, and Leif's name would forever be remembered as the hero who vanquished Thornheart and restored peace.

Chapter 9: Eternal Flame.

LEIF'S VICTORY OVER Thornheart was not without sacrifice. As he made his way back to Astrid, his heart was heavy with the knowledge that he had lost some of his closest allies in the battle. The once vibrant and lively realm now lay in ruins, a somber reminder of the cost of victory.

Leif's steps were slow and deliberate as he approached Astrid's side. She lay motionless, her body battered and broken from the battle. Leif's heart sank as he realised that she had fought valiantly alongside him, but had succumbed to her injuries.

Kneeling beside her, Leif gently cradled Astrid's lifeless form in his arms. Tears welled up in his eyes as he whispered her name, his voice filled with grief. He had grown to love Astrid deeply throughout their short life together, and now she was gone, lost to him forever.

In that moment, Leif made a solemn vow to honor Astrid's memory. He would continue his mission, not only to protect the realms but also to ensure that her sacrifice was not in vain. With renewed determination, he stood up, carrying Astrid's body in his arms, and began the long journey back to the gods' realm.

The gods, witnessing Leif's unwavering resolve and his grief-stricken determination, were moved by his devotion. They granted him a final gift, a token of their appreciation for his sacrifice and the love he had shown for Astrid. With their blessing, Leif's powers surged, becoming even stronger than before.

Leif's grief transformed into a burning fire within him, fueling his every step forward. He would not let Astrid's death be in vain. He would use his newfound power to protect the realms and ensure that no one else would suffer the same fate as she had.

As Leif returned to the gods' realm, he carried Astrid's body to a sacred resting place. He laid her to rest with utmost care, surrounded by flowers and adorned with the symbols of their journey together. Leif stood there for a moment, his hand resting on her grave, before he turned away, ready to face the challenges that awaited him.

From that day forward, Leif became a beacon of hope and strength, leading the charge against any threats to the realms. He fought with unwavering resolve and a burning fire in his heart, always carrying Astrid's memory with him. And though he could never forget the pain of her loss, he found solace in knowing that he was fulfilling his duty and protecting the realms they had fought so hard to save.

Leif's journey was far from over, and he knew that more battles awaited him. But with Astrid's spirit guiding him from beyond the grave, he faced each challenge with unwavering determination, knowing that he was not alone. Together, they would continue to protect the realms and honor the memory of their fallen comrades.

The Dragon Corp.

Chapter One: The Boy and the Dragon.

IN A SMALL VILLAGE on the edge of a great forest, lived a young boy named William. William was known throughout the village for his adventurous spirit and his love of nature. He would often spend long hours exploring the woods with his faithful dog, Rex. One day, as he was deep in the forest, he stumbled upon a small clearing where a magnificent creature lay sleeping. It was a dragon unlike any he had ever seen, with shimmering scales that glittered in the sunlight.

William approached the dragon cautiously, but it did not stir. He gazed at the creature in wonder for several minutes, marveling at its beauty. Suddenly, it opened its eyes and looked at him. William froze, unsure of what to do. But the dragon did not attack him. Instead, it just looked at him curiously.

For weeks, William visited the dragon every day, bringing it food and water. Eventually, the two developed a bond, and William discovered that the dragon was not the fearsome beast that everyone had thought it to be, but a gentle creature with a kind heart.

Chapter Two: Joining the Flying Dragon Corp.

ONE DAY, AS WILLIAM was sitting by the dragon's side, a group of dragon riders flew overhead. They were the Flying Dragon Corp, a group of elite warriors who rode on the backs of dragons. William watched in awe as they maneuvered through the air, their dragons soaring high above the treetops.

He had always been fascinated by the idea of riding dragons, and he realized that joining the Flying Dragon Corp was his life's dream. He knew that it was an unlikely aspiration, given his humble beginnings, but William was determined to make his dream a reality.

William went home that day and began to study everything he could about the Flying Dragon Corp. He read books, practiced sword fighting, and even learned how to speak Draconic, the language of the dragons. He spent every spare moment honing his skills, determined to become the best he could be.

Chapter Three: Training.

AFTER SEVERAL MONTHS of hard work, William's dedication paid off. The Flying Dragon Corp came to his village on a recruiting mission and William was one of the first to sign up. He was thrilled to be accepted, but he quickly realized that he had a long way to go.

Training with the Flying Dragon Corp was no easy task. Each day was filled with grueling exercises, dangerous missions, and intense combat training. But William was determined to succeed, and he threw himself into his training with everything he had.

At first, things did not go well. He struggled to keep up with the other recruits, and he made many mistakes. But he refused to give up. He listened carefully to his instructors, and he practiced constantly, always striving to be better.

Slowly but surely, he began to improve. His sword fighting became more precise, his riding more confident, and his physical fitness improved vastly. With each passing day, he drew closer to his goal of becoming a Dragon Rider.

Chapter Four: The First Flight.

AFTER MONTHS OF TRAINING, the day finally arrived. William was going to take his first flight on the back of a real dragon. His heart was pounding in his chest as he climbed onto the dragon's back, feeling the rough scales beneath him. He could feel the dragon's powerful muscles tensing beneath him, ready to spring into the air.

With a mighty leap, the dragon took off, climbing higher and higher into the sky. William held on tight, feeling the wind rushing past him as they soared through the clouds. He felt a rush of adrenaline as he looked down at the world below, seeing his village from a completely new perspective.

As they flew, William could feel the dragon responding to his commands. He felt a deep connection to the beast beneath him, and he realized that he and the dragon were working together as a team.

Chapter Five: The Battle.

AFTER MANY WEEKS OF flying, William was called upon to put his training to the test. The kingdom was under attack by a group of dark wizards, and the Flying Dragon Corp was called upon to defend it. William, along with his fellow Dragon Riders, flew into battle, their dragons breathing fire upon the enemy.

The battle was fierce, and William fought with all of his might to protect his kingdom. He dodged spells and swung his sword with precision, his dragon circling above him. He felt an incredible sense of power and freedom as he fought, knowing that he was doing something important and meaningful.

Despite the danger and the chaos, William felt a sense of calm. He knew that he was doing what he was meant to do, and he felt a deep sense of satisfaction in that knowledge.

Chapter Six: The Future.

YEARS WENT BY, AND William became one of the most elite Dragon Riders in the kingdom. He and his dragon were inseparable, and they went on many adventures together, seeing the world and defending the kingdom against all manner of threats.

William knew that he had found his true calling in life, and he felt grateful every day for the bond that he shared with his dragon. He knew that the training had been difficult, and the battles sometimes terrifying, but he also knew that it had all been worth it.

As he looked out over the kingdom from the back of his dragon, William felt a sense of peace settle over him. His life had been changed forever by his chance encounter with the dragon in the forest, and he knew that he would never be the same again.

Guardian of Arcadia

Chapter 1: The Enigmatic Awakening.

HE AWOKE IN A FOREST clearing, his naked form illuminated by the dappled sunlight that filtered through the towering trees. With his senses slowly returning to him, he found himself devoid of any belongings, save for a tattered cloak draped loosely around his shoulders and a bloodstained knife clutched tightly in his hand. Confusion clouded his mind as he tried to grasp the circumstances that had brought him to this enigmatic place.

The forest, lush and verdant, seemed to pulsate with an otherworldly energy, its ancient trees reaching towards the heavens as if yearning to touch the very fabric of the universe. Whispers carried on the wind, secrets whispered by the leaves as they rustled in a mesmerizing dance. It was as if the land itself held a deep-rooted knowledge, waiting patiently to be unraveled by those who dared to seek its mysteries.

He stood, his bare feet sinking into the soft earth, and surveyed his surroundings. The forest stretched out in every direction, an endless expanse of green that seemed to stretch on forever. The air hung heavy with the scent of damp moss and decaying leaves, mingling with the tantalizing aroma of wildflowers that bloomed in hidden pockets of sunlight.

As he ventured further into the heart of the forest, his senses sharpened, attuned to the subtle symphony of nature that surrounded him. The chirping of birds, the rustle of small creatures scurrying through the undergrowth, and the distant roar of a nearby waterfall created a harmonious melody that echoed through the ancient woods. It was a symphony that seemed to beckon him forward, urging him to uncover the truth that lay hidden within.

With each step, his mind raced, desperately searching for any fragment of memory that could shed light on his identity and the circumstances that had led him to this mysterious place. But the recesses of his mind remained shrouded in darkness, withholding their secrets as if protecting him from a truth too overwhelming to bear.

The cloak around his shoulders provided some semblance of comfort, its rough fabric shielding him from the cool breeze that swept through the forest. Its faded hues hinted at a history of its own, a tale that had been woven into its very fibers. Yet, even this humble garment provided no clues to his past, leaving him with nothing but questions and a growing sense of unease.

As he continued his journey, he became acutely aware of the ancient energy that permeated the forest. It was a force that seemed to vibrate through the very ground he walked upon, whispering secrets of forgotten times and long-lost civilizations. He could almost taste the weight of history in the air, a palpable presence that demanded his attention.

The trees, towering high above him, stood as silent sentinels, their gnarled branches reaching out like ancient arms, as if beckoning him closer. Their bark bore the scars of countless years, etched with the stories of generations past. It was as if these guardians of the forest held within them the wisdom of ages, waiting patiently for someone worthy to unlock their secrets.

With each passing moment, the sense of foreboding grew stronger, as if the very land itself was warning him of the dangers that lay ahead. But he was undeterred, driven by an insatiable curiosity to uncover the truth of his existence. He knew that within these depths, a profound revelation awaited him, one that would shape his destiny and unveil the enigma of his past.

With each step, he drew closer to the heart of the forest, closer to the answers he sought, and closer to the realization that his journey had only just begun.

Chapter 2: The Cave.

AS HE PRESSED ON, HIS footsteps falling softly on the moss-covered ground, his heart filled with a mixture of trepidation and excitement his attention is suddenly captured by a faint, ethereal glow emanating from a nearby cave. A mixture of curiosity and trepidation tugs at his mind, urging him to explore the depths of the mysterious cavern and unravel the enigmas that have plagued his thoughts for far too long. With each cautious step, his heart pounds in his chest, a symphony of anticipation and uncertainty.

His eyes fixated on the cave entrance, its dark opening beckoning him forward like a siren's call. The glow, ever so faint, dances and flickers, casting an otherworldly luminescence onto the surrounding vegetation. It is as if the cave holds a secret, a hidden knowledge that could provide the answers he seeks.

His mind races with questions that have plagued him for what seems like an eternity. Who am I? What is my purpose? What lies beyond the boundaries of my existence? He yearns for clarity, for a glimpse into the depths of his own soul.

Summoning his courage, he takes a tentative step towards the cave, his bare feet sinking deeper into the moist earth. The air around him feels charged with an unknown energy, a mixture of excitement and trepidation. He can almost taste the anticipation in the air, mingling with the scent of damp earth and the distant rustling of leaves.

As he moves closer to the cave's entrance, the glow intensifies, casting a warm, golden light onto his face. It is a comforting radiance, as if the cave itself is extending a welcoming embrace. His hesitancy begins to wane, replaced by an insatiable curiosity that propels him forward.

With every step, his senses heighten. The faint sound of dripping water echoes through the cavernous space, creating an eerie symphony that reverberates in his ears. The walls of the cave, adorned with ancient stalactites and stalagmites, seem to whisper ancient secrets, their rough surfaces begging to be touched and explored.

As he enters the cave, his eyes adjust to the dim light, revealing a vast expanse that stretches far beyond his line of sight. The glow, now more pronounced, emanates from an unknown source, casting intricate patterns on the cave walls. It is a mesmerizing sight, captivating his attention and drawing him further into the unknown.

With each step, his heartbeat quickens, his breath becoming shallow as he delves deeper into the cavern's depths. The air grows colder, wrapping around him like a chilling embrace. Yet, he presses on, determined to uncover the truth that lies within this mystical place.

As he ventures further, his mind becomes consumed with a sense of wonder and awe. The cave seems to pulse with life, its energy vibrating through his very being. It is as if the cave itself is a living entity, guiding him towards the answers he seeks.

His journey through the enigmatic cave is just beginning. With every step, he inches closer to the truth, his heart aching with a mixture of anticipation and fear. The glow, now a guiding light, leads him deeper into the unknown, promising revelations that may forever change his existence.

Chapter 3: The Hidden Chamber.

INSIDE THE DARK AND mysterious cave, a hidden chamber is unveiled, its entrance guarded by a veil of shadows. The walls of the chamber illuminated by some form of bioluminescence revealed a breathtaking sight. The chamber was adorned with intricate symbols and ancient artifacts, each holding a story of its own.

The walls, etched with faded drawings, depict scenes that seem to come alive in the flickering light. Battles between mighty warriors, their weapons clashing with a thunderous force, were frozen in time. The victorious celebrations that follow were captured with such vividness that one could almost hear the joyous cheers reverberating through the chamber. And amidst it all, mystical creatures, their forms both familiar and enigmatic, roamed freely, their presence adding an aura of enchantment to the chamber.

His eyes widen with awe, his heart pounding with excitement. A glimmer of recognition flickered within him, as if these drawings held a key to his forgotten past. Could it be possible that this ancient chamber, with its cryptic symbols and captivating illustrations, held the answers he has long sought?

He stepped closer to the walls, tracing the faded lines with his fingertips, hoping to unlock the secrets they held. As he did so, a surge of energy courses through his veins, as if the very essence of the chamber was awakening within him. Images flashed through his mind, fragments of memories long lost, teasing him with glimpses of a life he once knew.

The symbols etched onto the walls, once mere decorations, now took on a new significance. They seemed to whisper ancient wisdom, telling a story that only the worthy could decipher. His determination intensified, fueled by the belief that these symbols held the key to his true identity.

With a newfound purpose, he meticulously examined each artifact, searching for clues hidden within their delicate carvings. Ancient scrolls, adorned with faded ink, revealed fragments of forgotten texts, their meanings obscured by the passage of time. Intricate jewellery, once worn by revered figures, glimmered with a hidden power, waiting to be unleashed.

As he delved deeper into the chamber, he realised that he was not alone. The spirits of those who had gone before him seem to linger in the air, guiding him towards his destiny. Their whispers echoed through the chamber, urging him to press on, to unravel the mysteries that lay before him.

Days turn into nights, and nights into days, as he tirelessly pursued the truth hidden within the chamber's walls. His determination grew unyielding, his thirst for knowledge insatiable. He studied the drawings, the symbols, and the artifacts, trying to piece together fragments of his forgotten past.

One day as he stood before the chamber's grandest mural, tracing his fingers along the worn symbols, a surge of energy coursed through his body causing the engravings to come alive with an ethereal glow. The chamber itself seemed to tremble, as if awakening from a long slumber. And then, a voice, soft and yet commanding, echoed through the air, resonating deep within his soul.

"Seek the sacred stones," the voice whispered, its words carrying a weight of ancient wisdom, "for they hold the memories of your past."

In that moment, he knew that he had stumbled upon something extraordinary. The voice, so mysterious and yet compelling, ignited a fire within him, fueling his determination to uncover the truth that had been obscured by the sands of time.

Chapter 4: The Quest for Identity.

WITH A MIXTURE OF AWE and gratitude, he gazed upon the chamber one last time. He knew that this place, with its intricate symbols and ancient artifacts, would forever hold a special place in his heart. But he was determined to reclaim his identity, embarking on a perilous quest that would test his courage and resilience. Guided by the whispers of the wind and the ancient symbols etched in his mind, he set out to find the sacred stones, the key to unlocking the mysteries of his past.

His journey began through dense forests, where towering trees intertwined their branches, casting eerie shadows upon the forest floor. He followed the faint trail left by the stones, each step bringing him closer to the truth he so desperately sought. The forest seemed alive with secrets, and as he walked, he encountered wise hermits who had chosen to dwell in solitude. These hermits, with their weathered faces and eyes filled with ancient knowledge, imparted cryptic wisdom that fueled his determination.

With the hermits' words echoing in his mind, he ventured into treacherous mountains that pierced the sky. The air grew thin, and the winds howled relentlessly, threatening to push him off the narrow paths carved into the rocky slopes. Yet, he persevered, driven by an unyielding spirit. It was here, amidst the harsh elements, that he stumbled upon mysterious druids, guardians of ancient wisdom. They spoke in riddles and offered cryptic prophecies, their words like whispers carried by the wind. Though their messages were veiled, he understood that they held the keys to his destiny.

Descending from the treacherous mountains, he found himself in misty moors, where the ground beneath his feet seemed to shift with every step. The fog enveloped him, obscuring his vision and testing his resolve. But even in this disorienting landscape, he discovered kind-hearted villagers who recognized the fire in his eyes and the weight of his quest. They shared their humble homes and meager provisions, offering him respite and guidance. Their generosity fueled his determination, reminding him that he was not alone on this arduous journey.

As he pressed on, he faced daunting challenges that tested his physical and mental strength. Mythical creatures emerged from the shadows, their forms both beautiful and terrifying. They sought to deter him, to divert him from his path. But fueled by a newfound sense of purpose, he confronted these creatures with unwavering resolve. He learned to navigate the treacherous landscapes, to outsmart the cunning adversaries that crossed his path.

With each challenge overcome, his identity began to take shape. The whispers of the wind grew louder, the ancient symbols etched in his mind became clearer. The sacred stones, the very reason for his quest, were drawing near. And as he ventured further into the unknown, he realised that his journey was not just about reclaiming his identity, but also about discovering the strength and resilience that lay dormant within him.

The quest for the sacred stones had transformed him, molding him into a man who could face any obstacle with unwavering determination. Guided by the whispers of the wind and the ancient symbols that had led him thus far, he continued his perilous journey, ready to face whatever challenges awaited him. For he knew that the truth he sought was within his grasp, and that his identity would be reclaimed, not as a mere man, but as a warrior of the soul.

Chapter 5: The Sanctuary.

EACH STEP HE TOOK BROUGHT him closer to the sacred stones he sought, and with every passing day, his anticipation grew. He knew that these stones held the key to unlocking the memories of his past, a past that had been lost to him, but one that he yearned to reclaim.

Finally, his quest led him to a hidden sanctuary nestled high in the peaks of a majestic mountain range. The air here was crisp and filled with a sense of ancient power. As he entered the sanctuary, he felt a surge of energy envelop him, as if the stones themselves recognized his presence. The chamber before him was bathed in a soft, golden light, emanating from a pedestal at its center.

With bated breath, he approached the pedestal, his eyes fixated on the sacred stones resting atop it. They were unlike anything he had ever seen before, their surfaces shimmering with a kaleidoscope of colors, as if containing a universe within their depths. Each stone seemed to hold a story, a memory waiting to be unlocked.

As he reached out to touch the stones, a surge of anticipation coursed through him. He knew that this was the moment he had been waiting for, the culmination of his tireless search. With a gentle touch, he connected with the first stone, as his fingertips grazed the smooth surface, a surge of energy coursed through his veins. It was as if the stone itself had awakened something deep within him. In that instant, a flood of memories rushed into his consciousness, with each stone he touched, more memories were revealed, painting a vivid tapestry of his journey through time. Visions of ancient civilizations, long-forgotten battles, and lost loves flashed before his eyes. The stones were indeed vessels of memory, holding the stories of his past lives unraveling the mysteries of his existence and revealing his true identity.

He was not just an ordinary man, but the last of the ancient guardians. Chosen by fate, he bore the immense responsibility of protecting the land from an impending darkness that threatened to consume it whole. The weight of his destiny settled upon his shoulders, both daunting and empowering.

When he finally emerged from the sanctuary, he carried with him not only the memories of his past lives but also a newfound sense of purpose. The quest that had consumed him for so long had led him to a profound understanding of himself and his place in the world.

Chapter 6: A New Hope for Arcadia.

WITH THE STONES POWER surged within him, he was transformed into a beacon of hope for the people of Arcadia. He was no longer just a man; he had become the embodiment of their collective strength and resilience. The once scattered and fearful inhabitants would now find solace in his presence, knowing that their guardian had risen to lead them through the encroaching darkness.

Word of the guardian's awakening spread like wildfire, igniting a spark of hope in the hearts of the people. They had long yearned for a savior, someone who could rally them against the impending doom that loomed over their land. Now, with the guardian's true name echoing through the whispers of the wind, they found renewed courage to stand united.

Arcadia had always been a land steeped in legends and folklore, but this was no mere tale. The guardian's existence was a testament to the ancient prophecies that had foretold of a chosen one who would rise in their darkest hour. The people, once divided by their differences, now set aside their grievances, united in their shared purpose.

As the guardian stepped forward, the stones resonated with his every movement, amplifying his power. His presence alone commanded attention and respect, drawing all eyes towards him. The people, from the humblest farmer to the noblest warrior, looked upon him with awe and reverence.

In the days that followed, the guardian tirelessly traveled throughout the land, spreading the word of hope and rallying the people to prepare for the impending battle. He shared his knowledge, teaching them the ancient ways of combat and magic that had been passed down through generations. With each passing day, their resolve grew stronger, their spirits unyielding.

The guardian's unwavering determination and unwavering faith in their cause became a guiding light for all. He reminded them of their shared heritage, their deep connection to the land, and the strength that lay within each of them. No longer would they cower in fear; they would face the darkness head-on, armed with the knowledge that their guardian stood beside them.

The people of Arcadia, once resigned to their fate, now stood tall and resolute. They had found purpose in the face of adversity, and their guardian had kindled a fire within their hearts that would not be extinguished. Together, they would face the encroaching darkness, ready to fight for their land, their loved ones, and their future.

Chapter 7: The Darkness Within.

CALEB, THE MOST FEARED warrior in all of Arcadia, stood atop a hill overlooking the vast battlefield. His eyes scanned the horizon, taking in the sight of his army - a collection of trolls, dwarves, and ogres, all ready to fight alongside him. A formidable force of nature, he had risen to challenge the peace and harmony of Arcadia. Little did he know that a dark force was lurking within him, waiting for the perfect moment to take control. As the battle with the Guardian's army commenced, Caleb's heart pounded with anticipation. He unsheathed his sword, its gleaming blade reflecting the sunlight. With a mighty roar, he charged forward, his army following closely behind. The clash of steel and the cries of battle filled the air, but Caleb remained focused, his mind clear and determined.

However, as the battle raged on, a strange sensation began to creep into Caleb's core. It started as a subtle whisper, a voice urging him to embrace the darkness within. At first, he dismissed it as a trick of his imagination, a mere distraction amidst the chaos of war. But the voice grew louder, more insistent, until it became impossible to ignore.

Caleb's movements became more aggressive, his strikes fueled by an unnatural strength. His eyes, once filled with determination, now glowed with an eerie darkness. The warriors around him noticed the change, their gazes filled with a mix of fear and uncertainty.

The darkness within Caleb began to take control, twisting his thoughts and altering his actions. He fought with a ferocity that bordered on madness, his once calculated moves now reckless and unpredictable. The trolls, dwarves, and ogres, who had once trusted him implicitly, now hesitated to stand by his side. As the battle raged on, the Guardian's forces began to crumble under Caleb's relentless assault. The darkness within him seemed unstoppable, tearing through the guardians ranks with a merciless fury. But with each victory, Caleb's humanity slipped further away, replaced by a malevolent force that sought only destruction.

Chapter 8: The Final Confrontation.

THE AIR CRACKLED WITH tension as the guardian stood before Caleb, the embodiment of darkness, his heart pounding in his chest. Gripping his bloodied knife tightly, he could feel the power of the sacred stones coursing through his veins, empowering him for this climactic battle.

The darkness loomed over him, a formidable force that had plagued the land for far too long. It whispered sinister promises of destruction and despair, but he remained resolute, his determination burning brighter than ever. This was the moment he had trained for, the moment he had sacrificed so much for.

With a fierce battle cry, he lunged forward, his knife slicing through the air. Each strike was precise, fueled by his unwavering purpose. Caleb recoiled with each blow, the malevolent energy waning as the guardian chipped away at its power.

The ground trembled beneath their feet as the clash of their forces intensified. The sky darkened, as if mirroring the struggle unfolding below. The guardians every move was a testament to his unwavering will and the strength he had gained from the sacred stones.

As the battle raged on, sweat dripped down his brow, his muscles aching from the strain. Doubt tried to creep into his mind, but he pushed it aside, focusing on the task at hand. He knew that he was the only hope for the land, the only one capable of banishing this malevolent force for good.

With one final surge of energy, he delivered a devastating blow, his knife piercing through Caleb's heart. A blinding light erupted, illuminating the battlefield and dispelling the shadows that had plagued the land.

Silence fell upon the once chaotic scene as the darkness dissipated, leaving behind only a sense of relief and triumph. The guardian stood tall, his chest heaving with exertion, his eyes shining with the knowledge that he had emerged victorious.

The land, once shrouded in darkness, began to heal. The sun's rays broke through the clouds, casting a warm glow on the rejuvenated landscape. The people, who had lived in fear for so long, their faces now filled with hope.

As he surveyed the land, now free from the clutches of darkness, he couldn't help but feel a sense of fulfillment. The battle may have been won, but his journey was far from over. There were still challenges ahead, still battles to be fought. But armed with the power of the sacred stones and the unwavering support of those who believed in him, he knew that he would face whatever came his way with courage and determination.

And so, he set off into the horizon, ready to face the next chapter of his life, knowing that he had the strength to overcome any darkness that may come his way.

The Battle for Garondor.

Chapter 1: The Rivalry of Garondor.

IN THE LAND OF GARONDOR, where the steep cliffs wove a tapestry of rock and stone, there existed a delicate balance between three powerful clans. Each clan had their own unique characteristics, traditions, and territories. The centaurs of the Eredvin Plains were known for their swiftness, agility, and deep connection with the land. The dwarves of the Ironfist Valley were renowned for their craftsmanship, resilience, and unyielding loyalty to their kin. The ogres from the Norgul Depths possessed immense strength, formidable size, and a primal ferocity that sent shivers down the spines of all who encountered them.

Despite their differences, all three clans shared a common longing for dominance over Garondor. Centuries had passed since they first settled in their respective territories, and over time, tensions had grown. Each clan saw themselves as the true owners of Garondor, vying for control and superiority.

The centaurs, with their exceptional speed and knowledge of the land, felt that they were the rightful rulers. They believed that only they could fully harness Garondor's natural resources and protect its inhabitants. Skilled archers and seasoned riders, they roamed the vast Eredvin Plains, leaving no stone unturned in their quest for supremacy.

The dwarves, masters of stone and metal, held a different view. They believed that their craftsmanship and indomitable spirit made them the natural leaders of Garondor. Deep within the Ironfist Valley, they crafted mighty weapons and impenetrable armor, meticulously designed to defend their ancestral home and assert their authority over all.

On the other hand, the ogres, with their towering size and brute strength, had a more primal approach. They considered themselves the most fearsome clan and thought that sheer power alone was enough to claim Garondor as their own. Nestled within the treacherous Norgul

Depths, they lurked in the shadows, awaiting the perfect opportunity to strike and overpower their rivals.

As the rivalry intensified, occasional clashes erupted between the clans, resulting in battles that shook the very foundation of Garondor. The land itself bore witness to the countless conflicts, with scars etched upon its surface. The steep cliffs and intertwining valleys became the battlegrounds where the fate of Garondor would be decided.

Yet, amidst the turmoil of the clans' rivalry, whispers of unity and harmony began to echo among some of their members. Centaurs who appreciated the artistry of the dwarves and the strength of the ogres reached out to their rivals, craving a peaceful coexistence. Dwarves who admired the swiftness of the centaurs and the raw power of the ogres recognized the potential of combining their strengths. Even some of the ogres, touched by the craftsmanship of the dwarves and the connection to the land of the centaurs, started to question the eternal conflict.

In the land of Garondor, where the steep cliffs wove a tapestry of rock and stone, the clans continued their relentless pursuit of dominance. But as the simmering tensions threatened to consume them, the whispers of unity grew louder, offering a glimmer of hope for a future in which the power struggles would yield to cooperation. Only time would tell if Garondor would find peace and prosperity or descend further into chaos.

.Chapter 2: The Return of the Ancient Ogre King.

AS THE STARS GLITTERED in the serene skies, an ominous history was about to resurface. Morkram, The Ancient Ogre King, had awoken from his years of slumber, stirring ancient memories of darkness and despair. His name alone was enough to send shivers down the spines of those who had lived through his previous reign of terror.

In the age long past, Morkram was hailed as a creature of malevolent power, towering over the lands and striking fear into the hearts of all who crossed his path. He ruled with an iron fist, leaving destruction and chaos in his wake. His very presence cast a dark shadow that seemed to consume even the brightest of hopes.

The origins of Morkram's malevolence were shrouded in mystery. Legend spoke of a once noble and revered leader of the ogre race, who had succumbed to the corrupting power of forbidden magic. With each step deeper into darkness, Morkram transformed into an abomination, his soul twisted and tarnished by his insatiable lust for power. The ogre king's transformation drove even his most loyal subjects to fear and dread.

During his previous reign, entire kingdoms fell under Morkram's brutal rule. The once picturesque landscapes were scarred by his monstrous influence. Villages and towns were razed to the ground, leaving only ashes and echoes of despair behind. The people cowered in fear, forced to submit to the tyrant's whims or face his wrath.

But Morkram's reign was not without resistance. Brave warriors, desperate to free their lands from the grip of this malevolent tyrant, formed alliances and fought valiantly against him. They were driven by a collective determination to restore peace and harmony to the shattered realms.

After years of relentless battles and sacrifices, a coalition of heroes stood against Morkram in what would be known as the Final Battle. Legends were born as swords clashed and magic surged through the air. It was a battle of epic proportions, a clash between good and evil that would determine the fate of the world.

In the end, it was a combination of bravery, strategic brilliance, and a flicker of hope that led to Morkram's defeat. Disarmed and stripped of his power, the ogre king was sealed away in a tomb of magic, destined to slumber for eternity—or so they had hoped.

And now, centuries later, as Morkram's tomb lay broken and his consciousness reawakened, he hungered for revenge. The memory of his previous reign of terror drove him to reclaim his throne, as the stars glittered in the serene skies, the stage was set for a new era of conflict, where legends would be once again forged and destinies entwined in the face of an ancient malevolent power. The fate of the land hung in the balance, with the unwelcome return of The Ancient Ogre King.

Chapter 3: A Fragile Coalition.

IN THE FACE OF THE catastrophic awakening, Lonak, the strong and hotheaded leader of the centaurs, and Gruff SteelBeard, the wise and resolute chieftain of the dwarves, realized that their petty squabbles over territorial lines and mining rights were insignificant compared to the common enemy they now faced. This realization urged them to set aside their differences and join forces for the greater good.

At first, it was not an easy task for Lonak and Gruff SteelBeard to let go of their longstanding animosity towards each other. The centaurs and dwarves had been in conflict for generations, with bitterness and mistrust deeply rooted in their interactions. However, the devastating events of the catastrophic awakening shook their foundations and forced them to reassess their priorities.

Recognizing the gravity of the situation, Lonak and Gruff SteelBeard summoned their respective companions and convened a meeting at a neutral ground. Both leaders acknowledged the importance of putting aside their grievances and focusing on the common enemy that threatened their existence.

During the meeting, Lonak and Gruff SteelBeard saw a mutual determination in each other's eyes. They realized that by combining their forces, they could create a formidable coalition that would stand a chance against their shared adversary. It was in this moment that they forged an alliance that would change the course of their history.

Setting aside their personal pride, both leaders started working together to strategize and coordinate their efforts. They shared knowledge and resources, pooling their strengths and abilities to confront the common enemy head-on. Lonak's strength and ferocity complemented Gruff SteelBeard's strategic wisdom and resilience, making them a formidable pair in battle.

The centaurs and dwarves, witnessing their leaders' unity and commitment, were inspired to follow suit. They set aside their differences as well, recognizing that survival depended on their collective efforts. Together, they formed a powerful alliance, one that transcended the boundaries of their races and redefined their shared destiny.

As the story progressed, Lonak and Gruff SteelBeard's alliance became a symbol of hope for both the centaurs and dwarves. It demonstrated the positive impact of unity and collaboration in the face of adversity. Their example inspired others to put aside their differences and work towards a common goal, creating a sense of camaraderie and solidarity that would shape the course of their world.

Chapter 4: The Charge of Centaurs.

AS THE SUN BROKE OVER the horizon, painting the sky with hues of gold and pink, the day of reckoning had arrived. The field was alive with the sounds of weapons clanking, voices raised in chants, and the rhythmic heartbeat of anticipation. The warriors, both centaurs and dwarves, lined up side by side, their eyes fixed on the dark figure of Morkram and his formidable ogre legion.

Galloping forth, the centaurs embodied a fierce determination, their hooves thundering against the earth, sending clouds of dust swirling in the air. With their muscular upper bodies and equine lower halves, they were a force to be reckoned with. Each centaur wore a determined expression, their eyes gleaming with unwavering bravery.

Their leader, Lonak, a noble centaur with a regal mane and a glint of wisdom in his eyes, raised his mighty sword high above his head, commanding the attention of the entire army. His voice echoed across the battlefield as he bellowed a battle cry that resonated deep within the hearts of his warriors.

With a primal roar, the centaurs charged forward in unison, their bodies a blur of strength and power. The thunderous pounding of hooves and the snorts of determination filled the air, drowning out any other sound. The ground shook beneath them as they closed the distance between themselves and the ogres.

Arrows whizzed through the air, launched by the nimble dwarves standing shoulder to shoulder with their centaur allies. The arrows found their marks, striking down ogres with deadly precision. The centaurs, armed with spears and swords, clashed with the ogres, their fierce resolve unyielding.

As the centaurs engaged in close combat, their bravery shone like a beacon amidst the chaos. They fought with a ferocity born from a desire to protect their land and the ones they held dear. They displayed remarkable agility as they lunged at their foes, their hooves kicking and their weapons slicing through the air. The centaurs fought as one, seamlessly coordinating their movements and defending each other's backs.

They formed an impenetrable wall of bravery, refusing to succumb to the intimidation of the enemy. With every swing of their weapons, they carved a path through Morkram's ogre legion, not allowing fear or doubt to cloud their minds.

Despite the overwhelming number of ogres, the centaurs pressed forward undeterred. Their unwavering loyalty and unwavering faith in each other propelled them onward, their spirits unyielding. They fought fiercely, refusing to be subdued, their determination driving them to push past their limits.

Through their unmatched courage, the centaurs inspired awe and admiration on both sides of the battle. Their bravery etched in sweat and dirt on each face, they pressed on relentlessly, a shining example of heroism. The air crackled with the energy of their charge, infused with a sense of hope that the balance of power could be shifted in their favor.

As the day wore on, the centaurs continued their assault, never wavering in their devotion to their cause. They fought with an indomitable spirit, their eyes fixed on victory. The battle raged on, but the centaurs remained resolute, their courage burning brighter with each passing moment.

In the face of overwhelming odds, the centaurs had proven themselves to be a force that could not be easily overcome. Their battle-hardened hearts beat as one, their determination compelling them to fight until their last breath. They were champions of valor, embodying the truest essence of heroism.

And so, the centaurs charged onward, their determination to thwart Morkram and his ogre legion unfaltering. As the clash of steel reverberated across the battlefield, they stood tall, unyielding against the encroaching darkness, ready to fulfill their destiny and shape the course of the battle.

Chapter 5: Dark Magic.

THE OGRES ROARED AS they met the centaurs' charge, swinging their massive clubs and axes with brutal force. Many of the centaurs fell, their bodies crushed or severed by the ogres' weapons. But the centaurs did not falter, they fought with courage and skill, using their spears and swords to pierce the ogres' thick hides and vital organs. They also used their hooves to kick and trample the ogres, breaking their bones and skulls.

Morkram watched the battle from a hilltop, his eyes glowing with malice. He was not worried about the centaurs, he knew that his ogre legion outnumbered them by far. He was waiting for the right moment to unleash his secret weapon, a weapon that would turn the tide of the battle and ensure his victory. He smiled wickedly as he saw a large group of centaurs advancing towards his position, unaware of the trap he had set for them.

He raised his staff and uttered a dark incantation. A loud rumble shook the ground, and a huge fissure opened up beneath the centaurs' feet. The centaurs screamed as they plunged into the abyss, their cries echoing in the air. Morkram laughed maniacally, enjoying their suffering.

But his laughter was cut short when he heard another sound, a sound that filled him with dread. It was the sound of horns, horns that signaled the arrival of reinforcements. He looked up and saw a sight that made his blood run cold. A large army of dwarves had arrived on the battlefield, led by none other than Gruff Steelbeard himself. He wielded a sword that radiated with holy light, a sword that was said to be forged by the gods themselves.

Gruff Steelbeard raised his sword and shouted a battle cry that inspired his allies and terrified his enemies. "For freedom! For justice! For glory!" The army echoed his words and charged towards Morkram and his ogres, ready to join the centaurs in their fight against the dark lord.

Morkram felt a surge of fear and anger. He realized that he had underestimated his foes, that he had been too arrogant and overconfident. He knew that he had to retreat, to regroup and plan a new strategy. He cursed under his breath and ordered his ogres to follow him. He turned his back on the battlefield and fled, hoping to escape before it was too late.

The centaurs saw Morkram's retreat and cheered. They felt a new hope rising in their hearts, a hope that they could win this war and free their lands from Morkram's tyranny. They thanked Gruff Steelbeard and his army for their timely arrival. Gruff Steelbeard smiled and praised them for their bravery and valour.

Together, they pursued Morkram and his ogres, determined to end his reign of terror once and for all. As they marched on, they sang songs of victory and glory, songs that would be remembered for generations to come.

Chapter 6: The Pursuit to the Fortress.

AS THE SUN BEGAN TO set over the vast plain of desolation, the centaurs and dwarfs gathered their forces, determined to pursue Morkram and his ogres to his fortress. The alliance between these two unlikely groups had formed out of necessity, for they knew that only by working together could they hope to defeat the ogre king and put an end to his reign of terror.

With their weapons sharpened and their spirits high, the centaurs and dwarfs set off, their hooves and feet pounding against the barren ground. The centaurs, with their muscular torsos and powerful horse-like legs, galloped ahead, their bows and arrows at the ready. The dwarfs, short and stout, followed closely behind, their axes glinting in the fading light.

As they rode, the wind whispered tales of Morkram's cruelty, carrying the cries of the innocent victims he had enslaved. The centaurs and dwarfs knew that time was of the essence, for every moment they delayed, Morkram grew stronger and his fortress more impenetrable.

Guided by the centaurs' keen senses, the alliance tracked Morkram's path, following the trail of destruction left in his wake. The once vibrant landscape had been reduced to a desolate wasteland, with twisted trees and scorched earth as far as the eye could see. The air was heavy with an eerie silence, broken only by the distant howls of the ogres.

As they neared the fortress, the centaurs and dwarfs slowed their pace, their eyes scanning the horizon for any sign of Morkram's forces. The fortress stood tall and foreboding, its dark stone walls rising like a fortress of nightmares. It was surrounded by a moat of bubbling lava, a deadly barrier that seemed impossible to cross.

Undeterred, the centaurs and dwarfs devised a plan. The centaurs, with their agility and speed, would distract the ogres, drawing them away from the fortress. Meanwhile, the dwarfs would use their knowledge of underground tunnels to find a way to breach the fortress walls.

With their plan in place, the alliance split into two groups. The centaurs galloped towards the ogres, their arrows flying through the air, striking their targets with deadly precision. The ogres, caught off guard, roared in anger and charged towards the centaurs, their massive bodies shaking the ground beneath them.

While the centaurs engaged the ogres in battle, the dwarfs began their underground journey. They navigated through a labyrinth of tunnels, their torches casting eerie shadows on the damp walls. The dwarfs' determination never wavered, even as they encountered traps and obstacles set by Morkram to protect his fortress.

Finally, after what felt like an eternity, the dwarfs emerged inside the fortress walls. They quickly regrouped, their axes at the ready, prepared to face whatever awaited them. The fortress was a maze of dark corridors and hidden chambers, but the dwarfs were undeterred. They knew that their mission was not only to defeat Morkram but also to rescue the innocent souls he had imprisoned.

As dwarfs fought their way through the fortress, their determination grew stronger with each step. They could hear the cries of the captives, their voices filled with hope as they realised that help had finally arrived.

The battle raged on, the centaurs and dwarfs fighting side by side, their combined strength and skills proving to be a formidable force. Morkram's weakened forces were no match for the alliance and one by one, they fell before the might of the combined force.

Chapter 7: The End of Morkram's Reign.

FINALLY, THE DWARFS reached the heart of the fortress, where Morkram himself awaited them. The sorcerer, his eyes filled with malice, unleashed his dark magic, but the dwarves stood strong, their determination unwavering. Gruff Steelbeard led the charge, his sword cutting through the ogres like a hot knife through butter. His presence alone seemed to inspire, filling the dwarves with a newfound strength. The dwarves, stood their ground, their shields forming an impenetrable wall against the ogres' attacks.

Morkram, now cornered and desperate, attempted to conjure more dark magic to turn the tide in his favour. But his powers seemed to wane in the face of the might of the dwarves. His spells fizzled out, leaving him vulnerable and exposed.

Gruff Steelbeard, sensing Morkram's weakness, charged towards him with unwavering determination. The dark lord tried to defend himself, but his feeble attempts were no match for the dwarven warrior's skill and strength. With a mighty swing of his holy sword, Gruff Steelbeard struck Morkram down, ending his reign of terror once and for all.

The fortress fell silent, save for the heavy breathing of the victorious warriors.

The dwarves their bodies battered and bloodied, cheered as they saw their enemy fall. They had avenged their fallen kin and reclaimed their homeland. They rushed to SteelBeard, who lifted his axe in triumph. He had led them to victory, fulfilling his promise. He looked around at the faces of his comrades, feeling a surge of pride and gratitude.

He then turned his gaze to the throne of Morkram, where a large chest was hidden behind a curtain. He wondered what treasures awaited them inside. He motioned to his closest friend, Durgan, to join him.

Together, they approached the chest with curiosity and excitement. They lifted the lid and gasped at what they saw.

Inside the chest was a pile of gold coins, jewels, and artifacts of immense value. There were also weapons and armor of exquisite craftsmanship, some bearing the symbols of ancient dwarven clans. SteelBeard recognized one of them as the legendary Hammer of Tharim, a weapon that was said to have forged the first dwarven kingdom. He reached out to touch it, feeling a connection to his ancestors. He smiled and looked at Durgan, who nodded in approval. They had found more than they had hoped for. They had found their heritage. They called out to the others, inviting them to share in their discovery. The dwarves gathered around the chest, marveling at its contents. They celebrated their victory and their fortune, knowing that they had made history that day.

That's The dwarves and centaurs agreed to share the spoils of war, which included Morkram's treasure and his staff of black iron. The staff was a dangerous weapon, that could be used for good or evil. The dwarves and centaurs decided to split it in half, so that neither side would have the full power of Morkram. Gruff Steelbeard took the upper half of the staff, which had a metal claw that held a large ruby. Lanak took the lower half of the staff, which had a metal spike that could pierce through armor. They vowed to use their halves of the staff only for defense and justice, and never for greed or revenge.

They knew that this victory was not just theirs alone, but a victory for all those who had suffered under Morkram's dark rule.

They vowed to rebuild their lands, to heal the wounds inflicted by Morkram's tyranny, and to ensure that such darkness would never again take hold. They would stand as a testament to the power of unity and the indomitable spirit of those who fought for freedom and justice.

And so, the centaurs and dwarves returned to their respective lands, carrying with them the memories of their hard-fought victory. They would forever be bound by the bonds forged on the battlefield, their alliance a symbol of hope and resilience in the face of darkness. The songs of their triumph would echo through the ages, a reminder of the power of unity and the triumph of good over evil.

Marcus and Boudicca.

Chapter 1:

MARCUS, HAD BEEN A soldier in the Roman legion for several years, he had been trained to fight and conquer. He had seen his fair share of battles and had fought against many different enemies. His legion had just received orders from the Emperor Caesar to travel to Britannia and aid in the suppression of a local uprising, lead by a fierce warrior queen, known as Boudicca.

Marcus stood on the deck of the ship, overlooking the vast, stormy sea. He had been a soldier for many years, but this was his first time traveling across such a vast expanse of water. He couldn't help but feel a sense of excitement and trepidation as the wind howled around him, whipping his hair and his oilskin cloak into a frenzy. He had never felt quite so alone as he did at that moment, standing on the deck of the ship, surrounded by nothing but an endless expanse of water.

The journey proved to be long and arduous, with the rough seas throwing the ship back and forth, causing many of the soldiers to become seasick. Marcus had been fine until recently, at least until the stomach cramps hit him. He tried to ignore them at first, thinking they would pass, but soon he was doubled over in pain, retching continuously.

He knew something was seriously wrong when he passed out on the deck. The next thing Marcus remembered was waking up in a small cabin, feeling groggy and confused.

As he stirred, a gentle hand rested on his forehead. Marcus looked up and saw a man, a Greek he presumed, holding a mug of wine.

"Take it slow. You've been out of it for a while," said the man in a gentle accent.

Marcus nodded and took the mug, noticing the man's hands were quick and nimble as he tended to him. He realised that he was in the ship's sick bay, with the man in front of him being the ship's surgeon.

"What happened? How am I here?" Marcus asked, trying to piece together the last few hours.

"You passed out on the deck. Thankfully, one of your comrades helped you below deck, and I was able to treat you before your condition worsened," the surgeon, called Constantine, explained to Marcus that he had malaria and had almost died.

Marcus took a deep breath, relieved that he was alive, but still feeling weak. The surgeon handed him a small bowl of porridge, which Marcus ate slowly, savoring each spoonful.

Over the next few days, Marcus spent most of his time in the sick bay, recovering from his illness. Constantine tended to him with care, giving him medicines, ensuring that he was well-fed and keeping him company to lift his spirits. Slowly but surely, Marcus began to feel himself again.

As the ship finally approached the coast of Britannia, Marcus was ready to serve his duty. However, he knew that he owed his life to the ship's Greek surgeon, who had shown him true kindness during his darkest hours.

"Thank you," Marcus said, grasping the surgeon's hand as he left the sick bay.

"It was my duty. Take care, and may the Gods be with you in your battles," the surgeon replied with a warm smile.

Chapter 2:

THE ROMAN LEGION DISEMBARKED from the ship and began to march inland, their armor clanking loudly as they went. Marcus knew that they were in for a long and difficult campaign.

As they marched, Marcus couldn't help but marvel at the wild, untamed beauty of the landscape. The rolling hills and dense forests seemed to stretch out forever, and he could hear the distant cries of birds and animals echoing across the countryside.

But there was little time for sightseeing - the rebellion was spreading quickly, and the Roman legion had to move fast if they were going to quell it. Marcus's legion were assigned to a group of experienced soldiers who had been working to quell the uprising for several months. He quickly learned that the situation was far more complex than he had anticipated. The natives were fierce and determined, and their passion for independence was evident in their every action.

Despite the challenges, Marcus was determined to succeed in his mission. He worked closely with his fellow soldiers, learning everything he could about the local terrain and the tactics of the rebels. He was a fast learner, and his skills as a soldier quickly earned him the respect of his comrades.

Marcus and the rest of the legion were marching through the dense forest. They were a formidable force, well-disciplined and well-equipped, with years of training and experience under their belts.

As they marched, Marcus was deep in thought, considering the challenges that lay ahead. Little did he know that an even greater challenge was about to present itself.

Suddenly, the trees around them rustled, and before they knew it, the Roman legion was ambushed by a group of fierce warriors, led by none other than Queen Boudicca herself. Marcus had never been so afraid in his life, he had never faced such fierce warriors as these who were now surrounding him and his comrades.

The legionnaires fought valiantly, but they were vastly outnumbered and outmatched. Marcus had watched in horror as his friends and fellow soldiers were cut down one by one by the fierce warriors.

They quickly realized that their only chance of survival was to retreat and regroup. They turned and ran, pursued by the iceni warriors. Marcus felt a sharp pain in his leg and looked down to see an arrow lodged in his calf. He stumbled and fell, and his comrades urged him to keep moving.

"Go on without me," Marcus gasped. "I'll hold them off."

His comrades hesitated, but Marcus urged them to go. He knew that they needed to escape and bring back the intelligence they had gathered.

Marcus fought bravely, using his sword to fend off the iceni warriors. He managed to take down several of them before he stumbled and fell to the ground, and as he lay there, helpless, he saw a group of warriors coming towards him. looking at them with defiance in his eyes he said "If you are going to kill me, do it now. I would rather die than be a prisoner."

He felt a blow to the back of his head and everything went dark.

When Marcus woke up, he was a prisoner. He was tied up and his wound had been treated, but he was still in pain. Staring around he realised he was in the presence of queen Boudicca.

Chapter 3:

BOUDICCA WAS A TALL woman, with long red hair and piercing blue eyes. She wore a cloak made of animal skins, and carried a sharp-edged sword at her side. Marcus felt a shiver run down his spine as he looked at her, but he tried to keep his composure, knowing that any sign of weakness could mean death.

"Well, well," Boudicca said, as she approached him. "What do we have here? A wounded Roman soldier."

Marcus gritted his teeth, refusing to surrender to his fear. "I am a legionnaire," he said, his voice steady. "And I will fight for my people until my last breath."

Boudicca laughed, a sound that sent a chill through Marcus's body. "You Romans are so brave," she said. "But bravery won't save you now. You are my prisoner, and you will do as I say."

Marcus closed his eyes, preparing for the worst. But to his surprise, the queen ordered her warriors to take him back to the Roman camp, where he could receive medical attention. Marcus could hardly believe it - he had been spared.

As the warriors carried him, Marcus glanced back at Boudicca. He knew that she was a formidable opponent, a leader who inspired fear in her enemies. But he also couldn't help feeling a sense of respect for her. She was a warrior, just like him, and she fought for her people with every fiber of her being.

Chapter 4.

MARCUS GROANED IN PAIN as he lay on the bed in the Roman legion's camp. His wound had been treated, but it was still causing him discomfort. As a soldier, he knew that his duty was to get back on his feet and fight again, but his body needed time to heal.

Days turned into weeks and Marcus found himself growing restless. He missed being out in the field with his fellow soldiers, fighting for the glory of Rome. But he was stuck in the camp, under the watchful eye of the medic.

One day, while he was sitting outside trying to soak up some sunlight, he saw a girl walking towards him. She was a vision in white, with long blonde hair that cascaded down her back in loose waves. She was the captain's daughter, Rebecca.

Marcus had heard about Rebecca from some of the other soldiers. They said that she was beautiful, but also fierce and strong-willed. They told stories of how she had stood up to her father and the other captains, showing them that she was just as capable as any man in the legion.

As Rebecca approached Marcus, he couldn't help but feel a little intimidated. He sat up straighter, trying to appear as though he was not just a wounded soldier lying around.

"Hello," she said, smiling at him. "How are you feeling?"

"I'm doing alright," Marcus replied, trying to keep the pain out of his voice.

Rebecca sat down next to him and began to talk to him about the camp, asking him questions about his life before he joined the legion. Marcus found himself opening up to her, telling her things that he had never shared with anyone before.

Over the next few days, Rebecca would come and visit Marcus . Sometimes they would sit and talk, and other times they would play games. Marcus found himself looking forward to her visits, and the pain in his wound seemed to lessen whenever she was around.

As Marcus' wound began to heal, he knew that he would have to leave the camp soon and return to the field. He didn't want to leave Rebecca behind, but he knew that he had no choice.

On his last day in the camp, Rebecca came to say goodbye. She hugged him tightly, and Marcus felt a pang of sadness in his chest. He knew that he would never forget her.

Chapter 5.

MARCUS STOOD AT THE head of his Roman legion, listening intently as their commander outlined the mission they were about to undertake. They had been ordered to find the camp of Queen Boudicca, the infamous leader of the Iceni tribe, who had been causing trouble for Rome and its allies across the land.

Marcus knew that this was not going to be an easy task. Queen Boudicca was a fierce warrior and fought relentlessly for the freedom of her people. Her army was made up of battle-hardened warriors who knew the land better than any Roman soldier ever could.

But Marcus also knew that his men were some of the best soldiers in the Roman Empire. They had been trained to fight and win against any enemy, no matter how fierce they may be.

Their orders were simple: locate the camp of Queen Boudicca and capture her. This was easier said than done, of course. The Iceni were fiercely loyal to their queen, and would not surrender without a fight.

Marcus and his legion set out early the next morning, marching through the dense forests that surrounded Bodicca's territory. They moved in silence, taking care not to alert any of the Iceni warriors to their presence.

The Roman soldiers knew that they were vastly outnumbered by the Iceni, and they had to utilize every advantage they had if they were going to be successful.

They moved swiftly and silently, taking care not to leave any trace of their passage through the forest. They marched for hours, spotting the occasional sign that they were on the right track.

As the night settled in, Marcus ordered his men to halt and make camp. They set up watchtowers, dug trenches, and prepared for an assault from the Iceni.

The night was dark and quiet except for the occasional sound of an owl or rustle of leaves. Markus felt a deep sense of apprehension; he knew that anything could happen that night.

As the night wore on, Marcus remained vigilant, keeping a watchful eye on his surroundings. He couldn't shake off the feeling that the Iceni were watching him.

Just as the first light of dawn began to pierce the darkness, Marcus and his legion set out again, making their way closer and closer to the camp of Queen Boudicca.

After a few more hours of marching, the Roman soldiers came upon a clearing. Marcus knew that they had to move quickly if they were going to find the Iceni camp.

He ordered his men to spread out, searching carefully for any sign of the enemy. After a few tense minutes, a scout spotted smoke rising in the distance. Markus knew that the Iceni camp was close. Finally, they reached the outskirts of the camp. Marcus ordered his men to set up a perimeter and prepare for battle. He knew they needed to strike fast before the iceni had a chance to react.

They launched a surprise attack on the camp, catching the rebels off guard. The two armies clashed in a fierce battle, and Marcus fought with all his might. He knew that the outcome of this battle would determine their fate.

Boudicca was a fierce and determined fighter who would not be intimidated by the might of Rome. Despite her bravery, however, the iceni were no match for the well-trained Roman troops.

As the Romans swept through the camp, Marcus and his men took as many prisoners as they could find. Among those captured was Boudicca herself. Marcus was struck by her beauty and her courage, even as he knew that she would be punished severely for her resistance.

Chapter 6.

OVER THE NEXT FEW DAYS, Marcus watched as Boudicca was interrogated and punished for her defiance. Despite her suffering, she refused to back down or to submit to her captors.

As the days passed Marcus began to see her as more than just a prisoner, but as a person with her own thoughts and feelings. He admired her strength and courage, and he could see that she was not just a barbarian, but a leader who cared deeply for her people. Marcus began to understand the pain and suffering that the Romans had caused her people. He began to question his loyalty to Rome and the violence that he had been trained to inflict. He wondered if there was a better way to live, one that did not involve conquering and subjugating others.

Eventually, Marcus knew that he could no longer be a part of the Roman army. He could not continue to conquer and oppress Boudicca and her people, And he made the difficult decision to help her escape. He recruited a small group of fellow legionaries who were sympathetic to his cause. Together, they formulated a plan to rescue the queen.

Chapter 7.

THEY DEVISED A PLAN that would involve infiltrating the camp and rescuing the queen under the cover of darkness. They knew that it would be risky, but they were willing to take the chance.

As the night grew darker, Marcus and his comrades crept towards the Roman camp, moving silently and cautiously. They managed to slip past the guards and make their way towards the queen's cell.

They moved quickly and quietly towards the queen's cell. When he finally spotted her, his heart sank. She looked exhausted and defeated, her once-strong spirit broken by the harsh conditions of her captivity.

Marcus and his team quickly freed the queen and led her out of the camp. They moved swiftly, knowing that they could be caught at any moment. But luck was on their side, and they managed to escape

but they could hear the sound of Roman legionaries pursuing them. They knew that they needed to move quickly, or they would be caught.

Suddenly, Marcus spotted a hidden trail that led into the forest. He knew that this was their only chance to escape. He quickly signaled to the others, and they followed him down the path.

The trail was narrow and steep, but they pressed on, driven by their determination to save the queen. As they ran, they could hear the Roman soldiers getting closer, but they refused to give up.

Finally, after what felt like an eternity, they burst out of the forest and onto an open plain. The moon had risen high in the sky, and they could see the Roman soldiers still pursuing them in the distance.

As they fled Marcus and Boudicca exchanged a look of mutual respect and gratitude. Marcus knew that he and his comrades had risked everything to help her, but he felt that they had made the right choice. He had found a new purpose and a new sense of belonging in Boudicca's struggle against the Romans.

From that day on, Marcus fought alongside Boudicca and her warriors, using his knowledge of Roman tactics and his own skills as a soldier to help them in their battles. He became a trusted member of Boudicca's inner circle, respected for his bravery and his loyalty.

Together, Marcus and Boudicca led their warriors in a fierce struggle against the Romans, fighting for the freedom and independence of their people. Marcus had found a new home and a new family in Boudicca's army, and he knew that he would never go back to the life he had known before.

Don't miss out!

Visit the website below and you can sign up to receive emails whenever George Gentle publishes a new book. There's no charge and no obligation.

https://books2read.com/r/B-A-COLRB-MMFQD

BOOKS 2 READ

Connecting independent readers to independent writers.